bad machinery

THE CASE OF
THE UNWELCOME VISITOR

ONI PRESS

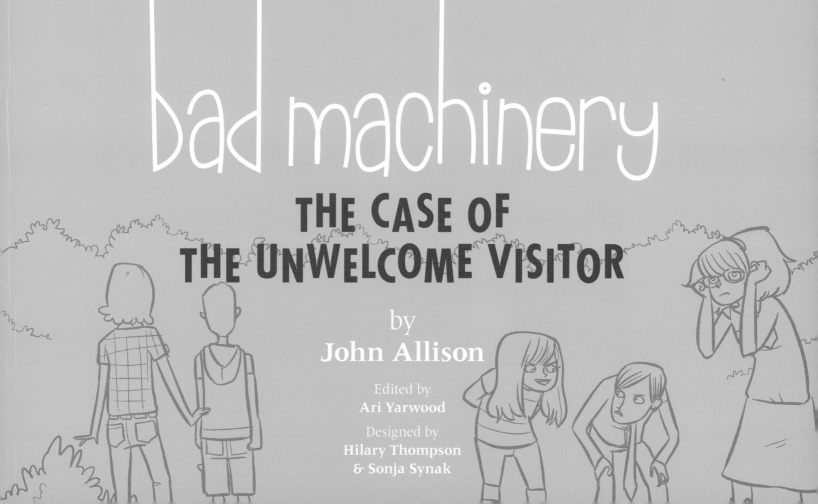

bad machinery

THE CASE OF
THE UNWELCOME VISITOR

by
John Allison

Edited by
Ari Yarwood

Designed by
Hilary Thompson
& Sonja Synak

PUBLISHED BY ONI PRESS INC.

founder & chief financial officer **Joe Nozemack**
publisher **James Lucas Jones**
v.p. of creative & business development **Charlie Chu**
director of operations **Brad Rooks**
director of publicity **Melissa Meszaros**
director of sales **Margot Wood**
marketing design manager **Sandy Tanaka**
special projects manager **Amber O'Neill**
director of design & production **Troy Look**
senior graphic designer **Hilary Thompson**
graphic designer **Kate Z. Stone**
junior graphic designer **Sonja Synak**
digital prepress lead **Angie Knowles**
executive editor **Ari Yarwood**
editorial director of licensed publishing **Sarah Gaydos**
senior editor **Robin Herrera**
associate editor **Desiree Wilson**
administrative assistant **Alissa Sallah**
logistics associate **Jung Lee**
warehouse assistant **Scott Sharkey**

onipress.com
facebook.com/onipress
twitter.com/onipress
onipress.tumblr.com
instagram.com/onipress

First Edition: November 2016
Pocket Edition: October 2018

ISBN 978-1-62010-343-6
eISBN 978-1-62010-352-4

Printed in China.

Library of Congress Control Number: 2018940559

1 2 3 4 5 6 7 8 9 10

The Case of the Unwelcome Visitor

20

The Case of the Unwelcome Visitor

The Case of the Unwelcome Visitor

54

Slim jim stopped by slim Jim

'NIGHT HERO' APPREHENDS CAR THIEVES

by ERIN WINTERS
Staff writer

AN ATTEMPTED car theft on Mondale Street in Wefton was stopped in the early hours by

describing the Night Hero as "the sort of man we've needed around here for years - God

NOTORIOUS DRUG CORNER CLEARED BY 'NIGHT HERO'

"Everybody's going to get well," says local residents' association

by ERIN WINTERS
Staff writer

Night Hero punishes sick youths

WAR MEMORIAL VANDALS ARE BROUGHT TO SWIFT JUSTICE

by ERIN WINTERS
Staff writer

VAGRANTS DRIVEN FROM UNDER PARK BRIDGE OVERNIGHT

Downtown hell-zone now popular with dog walkers; artisan cupcakery to open Thursday

by ERIN WINTERS
Staff writer

LOCAL OFFICIALS are at a loss to ex-

possibility that the Night Hero was part

The Case of the Unwelcome Visitor

The Case of the Unwelcome Visitor

The Case of the Unwelcome Visitor

During a recent visit to local junk-hole "Help The Wretched", I was lucky enough to find a copy of Don Gravy's autobiography — SING SOFTLY TO ME, SWEET WIND. Oh, what a book. Don is lots of things in this book but modest is not one of them. Here are a selection of my favourite pages which will take you deep within the mind of one of Tackleford's most "beloved" entertainers.

Charlotte Grote,
Keane End, Tackleford

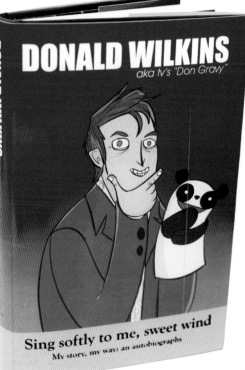

Extracts reproduced by kind permission of D. Wilkins Press

SCHOOLDAYS

I suppose I was a happy child. I did the things other kids did - I ran around, I hid, I kicked a ball, I scuffed me knees. But England was very different in the Seventies. Nowadays, no one says boo to a kiddie without being hauled up before before the judge for cruelty. Back then, children were seen and not heard. We had corporal punishment, and we were glad of it. Some schools had the slipper, others the cane, some the belt. If you did something wrong, someone twice your size was going to whack you. It wasn't unusual for a lad to leave school at 18 with buttocks that resembled a transit map.

At Coward Cross Primary School however, our headmistress, Mrs Thomas, was "modern". She didn't believe in striking a child. I found out later it was because she had weak rotator cuffs in her shoulders, and couldn't achieve a decent blow without a 20-yard run-up, which the layout of her office prevented. At Cross Primary, we had "the desk".

School desks had, traditionally, been single-seat wooden tables with a compartment and a lid. But a new broom was sweeping though the school system, and these had been set aside for Formica-topped tables where we sat in groups. One old, wooden desk remained in each classroom however. And if you misbehaved, you went in it. I went in it almost every week. It wasn't that I was naughty, so much as I couldn't stop talking.

The desk was a wicked thing to do to a child. As a five year old, it was almost funny to be shut inside the wooden container for half an hour. At six, a little tighter. At seven, it took a real squeeze to get your knees in. At eight and nine, the heaviest member of the class might be invited to sit atop the desk lid to compress your straining form into the ink-stained void. By ten and eleven, most kids knew to keep their noses clean. But not me. I will never forget the afternoon when, after loudly announcing that I had not enjoyed my lunch that day (Spam fritters and cabbage), being stuffed into the desk, which was then lashed closed with bungee cords. The wood split, and I burst forth with an explosive fervour only aided by the cabbage-driven flatus of my dreadful dinner.

9

SCHOOLDAYS

By fourteen I was done with school. I looked at the sad, tired faces of the teachers and knew I was best off out of there. I bunked off more than I showed up but, by the time I was meant to be sitting exams at fifteen, they weren't sending anyone out to look for me any more. I spent my mornings down by the canal with my metal detector, and the afternoons in the pub, listening to the drunks tell their stories.

There was no way I was missing the last week of school, though. "Muck-up week" they called it. Every year, people would go crazy with pranks and jests on a grand scale. There were legendary tales of the Physics master who came out at the end of the day to find a live wolf in his car, the head of French, who went home for the summer unwittingly (and legally) married to the school ferret, and the time five enterprising youths managed to sneak a minky whale into the school pool. I just wrote the word "PLUMS" onto the canteen wall with purple spray paint. They never caught me.

Before we left on that final day, the Headmaster sat down those of us not going on to college for a "little chat". I'll never forget his words.

"Boys, not every one of us is meant to be something. Some are bound for greatness. Others are more like the polystyrene peanuts that provide ballast for a crystal vase in transit. There is nothing glamorous about the polystyrene peanut, but without it, the beautiful vase would arrive cracked."

"You're cracked, mate," I said, baring my bottom to general mirth.

As I walked free of the school gates one last time, I was full of dreams, big dreams. I wasn't going to work in a factory or apprentice as a plumber like the other lads leaving. I was going to be somebody. I knew I could make people laugh - that was my gift. People had been laughing at me since I was a boy. If they weren't laughing as I entered a room (and they often were), they were laughing as I left it. I had a destiny, and it didn't involve canning peas at H. Percy's Pulse Works.

PEAS FOR BREAKFAST, LUNCH AND TEA

The best thing about working at the pea and bean canning factory, or rather, "H. Percy's Pulse Works", was that there were a lot of places that you could have a nice sleep. It wasn't unusual to turn on the labelling machine in the morning to hear the sudden howl of a night shift worker who'd tucked himself in for a little shut-eye behind the main piston. I was a natural at the factory, much as I proved to be in everything else I've done in life. There were no awards for doing the job right, but it was clear from the silent respect of my colleagues on the canning line that I was a rising star in the field, and would probably have been running the factory by Christmas had fate not come calling.

In common with many British factories at the time, H. Percy had an in-house radio station, broadcasting to the workers to keep spirits up. They'd play top 40 hits, oldies, and take requests. Mornings were hosted by Big Marjorie Jackson, while afternoons were introduced by "Captain" Ken Mather. The night shift (or "quiet storm") was a smooth treat played in by Wendell Q. Christopher, dripping with white gold. This three had held sway over the radio station since 1973, and might have continued to do so had Ken and Wendell not come to blows over Big Marjorie's affections, following the disintegration of her marriage.

So it was, one fateful day, the factory's afternoon and midnight DJs grappled for Marjorie's love on a footbridge over the mushy pea vats. So it was, both tumbled into the green miasma and were swiftly consumed. So it was, Big Marjorie went into seclusion. And so it was that the factory, once filled with song, now lay silent, day and night.

Morale collapsed. Work accidents reached epidemic levels. There was a finger lost most days. Management was in crisis. But who would fill the DJ booth? The fateful seat was still warm, and few wanted to risk that cursed gig. I marched up to Hamilton Percy Sr's office, and knocked on his door.

"I'll play the records, Mr Percy," I said. "I have a good understanding of reggae, punk, new wave, soul, smooth jazz and skiffle, and I believe no further lives will be lost." He said yes.

RADIO DAYS

As Alison St Clair breezed into the studio, every head turned. 1987's biggest pop star, near enough for me to reach out and touch! To think that a year ago, I'd been spinning "Touch Me Somewhere Sentimental" by Grassy Knoll for the ladies on the factory floor, and now I was playing songs for the whole Tackleford and Wendlefield Valley on Puddle FM. Alison was gorgeous, dressed head to toe in leopardskin and polyurethane. Her perfume was like a drug. And by the time her top ten hit "Monkey Around" stopped playing, I was going to have to interview her, live on the air. Bright red and flustered, I tried to make small talk.

"Did you get the train here?" I asked, trying to get my notes in order.

"I take helicopters, darling," she said, her deep hazel eyes cutting into me. "Everywhere. I'm a *star*."

Well, I felt like a prize prat. A wally. Of course she took helicopters everywhere. As I tried to recover my train of thought, I head the last notes of "Monkey Around" fade out.

"Ladies and gentlemen, I'm here with Alison St Clair, and I have to say, she's lookin' gorgeous as ever. Alison's playing the Tackle Valley Stadium tonight, and I'm sure all your fans want to know, what will you be wearing?" My question hung in the air for a second. It didn't half sound stupid. Alison parted her cherry lips.

"Very little, darling. As ever." Well! If I'd been struggling before, I was a man lost at sea now. I stammered out a few more questions, before Ms St Clair placed a gloved hand on my arm.

"Don, I have something for you." She reached into the folds of her leopard cape, and produced a seven-inch single. "This is my new record. I cut it yesterday with Nigel Swann at Royal Records. It's called "Thigh Highs (All Night)". I'd like you to be the first person to play it."

Five minutes later, as Alison was being swept out of the room by her manager, my producer Felix dashed in, frantic.

"Don, mate, they cut to national transmission halfway through your interview. You've just been heard by 40 million people."

A NATIONAL MAN

6

"Wilkins, thanks for coming in." Johnny Beerling, the controller of BBC Radio 1, cut an imposing figure, his hair like whipped ice cream atop a waffle-brown facial cone. He'd just returned from two weeks in Corfu. "I'm going to cut to the chase. We've offered Bates the breakfast show, and he said no. Doesn't want to give up the Golden Hour. So we'd like you to do it. What do you say?"

The Radio 1 Breakfast Show! The most listened-to radio programme in Britain! If you'd told the lad dreaming in his bedroom on a council terrace in Tackleford that in four years he'd be offered the top job on the nation's airwaves, well, I dare say he'd have fallen off that bed, perhaps awkwardly, maybe damaging his body in such a way that he would have been unable to have become one of the country's top disc jockeys.

Such are the perils and paradoxes of time travel, which sadly there is little scope to explore in this chapter. The greats that had filled the chair before me, great, unimpeachable men like Noel Edmonds, Mike Read and Mike Smith, booming voices that lifted the hearts of mums, dads and kids on the school run, lifted sleepy heads from the cereal bowl, playing the power hits that propelled lonely singletons from their beds to the workplace. To be such a vital cog in the national machine wasn't just an honour, it was a privilege. Beerling's breath was bated. He fingered his cravat impatiently. "Come on man. What do you say?"

"Radio's dead, Johnny," I sneered. "I've been asked to do telly. No one listens to the radio any more. Not interested."

A NATIONAL MAN

As a junior presenter on BBC 2's "Talkabout", my duties were limited, but that suited me fine. A couple of man-on-the-street interviews per show, in-studio pieces when required, and occasional hosting duties when Carol Beffin or Lord Maudsley were away. I was busy with family duties. Marta and I had married after a whirlwind romance, and almost nine months to the day after our wedding, Hunter Hawksley Wilkins was born.

My son was, and is, everything to me. But the late nights were hell. Hunter would wake every twenty minutes, demanding to be fed or changed, and Marta insisted we use the Polish technique, where the father attends to all the child's needs after 6.30pm. As a result, I was surviving on around two hours' sleep a night. Some nights, the only thing that would pacify our sweet lad was his panda glove puppet, Simon. The only drawback to Simon was that he had to "hug" Hunter, which required my hand. As soon as my grip slackened, our son would begin to cry.

In mid-July 1989, I was scheduled to host Talkabout while Lord Maudsley went on a shooting holiday in Norfolk. But on that fateful day, I fell asleep giving my boy a "Simon hug", my arm stretched awkwardly into the crib for hours. Bleary and confused, I was woken mid-afternoon by the telephone.

"Don, where are you?" came our producer's voice. "You should have been in make-up fifteen minutes ago!" Fortunately, our home was a short run from BBC Broadcasting House, and I somehow managed to make it on air in time, in the clothes I had been wearing the previous day. I read the autocue. "Welcome to Talkabout, I'm Don Wilkins. On today's show, a consumer report on lethal black market skateboards, and more on the scandal of Britain's collapsing hospitals."

Every pair of eyes was trained on me. People seemed locked in a state midway between amusement and horror. Carol turned to me, ignoring the autocue. "Don, is there something you'd like to tell us?" She pointed at my hand. The panda was still on it. I was mortified. But with the composure that defines me as a person, I answered her. "This... is Simon. Say 'hello', Simon."

SIMON SAYS

After a year of the "Don Gravy & Simon Show", things began to get a little out of hand - if you'll pardon my joke. We were on telly every week, in the gap between kiddies' TV and the news. Everyone saw it. There were only four TV channels back then, and two of them were terrible. Pretty girls would stop me in the street and give me their telephone numbers. Builders would shout "WHERE'S SIMON?" when I nipped out to the shop for a bag of crisps. I never had to buy a drink in a pub, never had to pay for a cab. The world stopped feeling real. For an appearance in Aldershot, a helicopter was chartered. I thought back to Alison St Clair... who's the big star now?

But I wasn't going to let it go to my head. You can take the lad out of Tackleford, but you can't take Tackleford out of the lad. I might have been getting my clothes made bespoke rather than off the peg, but that didn't make me fancy. I may have been dining at London's best restaurants and private clubs rather than eating a fish and chip supper from newspaper, but it's all just grub when it comes down to it. I may have had a cook, a cleaner, a maid and a driver, but I knew their names. You can't let that stuff go.

The peak of these crazy days came at the 1994 Royal Variety Performance. The Queen was there, and Prince Phillip, in the royal box, and I was booked to perform. Well, I put on quite the show. Simon had the kids in stitches, and the grown-ups too. Her Majesty was dabbing the corner of her eye and even Phil was smirking. After I performed, there was a knock on dressing room door. It was a royal footman, in full regalia - braid, medals, spurs and knee-boots. "Her Majesty Queen Elizabeth II requests the pleasure of your company at Buckingham Palace this evening." And so it was that a boy from the smoky streets of West Yorkshire found himself at a right royal lock-in with the Windsors - with the Queen Mother holding court - and the gin bottle - at a fully stocked wet bar. Modesty (not to mention the Official Secrets Act) does not permit me to recount the goings-on that night, but suffice to say that we were late to bed that night, with sore heads beneath the crown, the following morn.

TROUBLE IN PARADISE

They say it's a good life if you don't weaken, but alas, I've had a few slips along the way. My Dad, Paul, was a decent man, every day he left the house for Tackleford General Hospital, where he mopped floors, emptied bedpans, and kept his head down. It wasn't the sort of life you'd call glamorous. But in the pub at night, he shone. Paul could talk a blue streak and had charisma a mile wide. While Mum gave us kids our baths and our tea, he'd laugh the evening away over six or seven pints of heavy.

Now, Dad was kind, and we loved him. But we weren't the only ones. I remember the first time I saw my father with one of his "girlfriends". He was kissing Jacqueline Foster from the butchers, him with a leg of lamb under each arm, her still astride the shop bike. I saw him, he saw me, and I was red raw with rage. How could he step out on my beloved Mum? He ran after me and said words I'd never forget. "Son, your mother and me are solid as a rock. But I've got a lot of love to give, and it would be a crime not to share it." I nodded dumbly, and swore I would never be like him. Never would I cheat.

So why was I at Grimsby's leading French restaurant, The Kitty, with X, one of television's most recognisable beauties? Even in our secluded both, both of us knew we could be caught at any time - and her married to Y, her daytime sofa co-host and notorious brawler. Both our hearts were beating like drums.

"You complete me, Don," she said breathlessly, unloading an oyster into her Cupid's Bow mouth. "I've never felt more alive, being here with you now."

"And you I, X", I replied, "no woman has ever filled me with such divine fire." Her diamond necklace glittered in the candlelight, scattering her bosom with a thousand points of light. I knew that what I was doing was wrong, that Marta was at home in our Mayfair home while I played it fast and loose in "the Monte Carlo of East Yorkshire." But as it turned out, I was my father's son. And I never understood Paul Wilkins better than at the moment X took my hand and led me from the restaurant into the fishy night air. Oh X. Oh *Grimsby*.

PARADISE LOST

As the third dinner plate shattered around my ears, I realised that Marta and I had problems that a £5 bunch of flowers and a box of Terry's All Gold wouldn't solve. And there it was on the cover of today's News Of The World, in glorious black and white. "SHARON: TV LOVE RAT DON GRAVY ROMPED WITH ME WHILE HIS WIFE HAD SHINGLES".

"It's a misunderstanding!" I shouted, dodging shards of exploding porcelain. "We didn't really romp! There was a little light horseplay that got out of hand, a moment of weakness, maybe some shennanigans!" Marta didn't seem interested in the semantics of the matter. And who was I trying to kid? I'd got sloppy. There was a void at the centre of myself that I tried to fill with showgirls, luxury desserts, and sweet champagne wine. My chickens had come home to roost, and by the end of the night, this old fox was out of the henhouse.

What had first drawn me to Marta? As a judge on the Miss Rutland Competition panel I'd watched her parade, of course, but she wasn't a piece of meat to me, a trophy. I loved her mind. And what a mind. Unfortunately, that ingenuity was now put to work as she systematically destroyed every single one of my possessions in an orchestrated chain reaction that most closely resembled a Domino Rally.

As my 1971 MGB sports car careened into my collection of Fabergé eggs, the wreckage of which she then swept into to swimming pool, before setting the curtains on fire, I was struck dumb with the same admiration that had always been the foundation stone of our union. Sadly that speechlessness left me unable to intervene when she drove our spotless vintage Land Rover into our garden gazebo, which she'd filled with all my golf equipment, my awards, and the certificates for my shares, stocks and bonds. The car's engine exploded. The fire brigade were called. Marta turned to me, triumphant. "I am now going to my mother's. She is, coincidentally, an excellent divorce lawyer."

At that moment, the telephone rang. It was my agent, Suzanne. "Don, the BBC want to see you," she said. "They're... not happy."

12

They say that in showbusiness you should be nice to people on the way up, because that way they'll be nice to you on the way down. Now, I wasn't always an angel backstage. I worked hard, and expected the people around me to work hard too. So I made a few make-up girls cry. So I fired a few managers. So I spread the odd rumour about fellow presenters that might seen them swiftly removed. Of course I did. It was the Nineties, everyone was at it. I gave the little people jobs, the least they could have done was to be grateful.

So when Lord Montague called me into his grand office at the BBC, I expected a ticking off over the newspaper stories. A slap on the wrist. I'd given them ratings. I'd given them *magic*. They gave me my cards. The Mr Gravy And Simon show was cancelled.

"You can keep your stinking job," I told Montague. "I'll take Simon to ITV. That's where the real money is anyway." Then I bared my bottom to him, before taking my leave. Sometimes the old ways are the best.

Well, as it turned out, ITV *was* where the real money was. And they were keeping hold of it. No one wanted a kids' TV presenter who cheats on his wife and leaves his children without a father. I went to Channel 4. They offered me a late night slot. I told them, stick your graveyard shift, I'm going to satellite TV. Well, I did. And they told me that no one wanted a "puppet act" any more, television had moved on. It was all about "youth" and "edge", and I had neither. I was 41 years old, and I was on the scrapheap.

It turned out that no-one wanted TV's Mr Gravy. I couldn't go back to radio with Simon - he didn't speak! I just waggled his hands about and made him nod. After a humiliating meeting at Puddle FM (now re-branded as "Stride - News, Sport & Talk"), I realised that it was all over.

So I walked down to the river with Simon. Simon, who had taken me to my fortune. I placed the puppet over my hand, as I had done so many times before. Sweet Simon, who had never let me down. His sightless black plastic eyes stared up at me as if to say, "what now Don? What now?" And I could take it no more. I rained blows down upon that panda, cursing him, cursing fate. Every blow, a strike against my own right hand. When I could take it no more, I cast Simon into the water and watched his furry body sink into the murk. It was my lowest moment. My right hand, now bare, was black and blue.

I must have walked along the river bank for miles, plagued with the most desperate thoughts. Should I throw myself into the deep? Go up into the hills and live as a hermit? Or retrain as a chartered accountant and open up a high-street storefront, eventually building up a healthy clientele? All of these prospects seemed so bleak that I could not, would not countenance them.

And then I started up the hill back to Keane End, and the old Peas And Beans sign caught my eye. If there was one thing I knew how to do, it was can peas. Of course, there would be a healthy helping of humble pie to swallow, but nothing goes better with pie than peas. I knew that much.

I reached the old factory gates, and watched the day shift leave and the night shift roll in. This wouldn't be forever. Just a stop along the way, before I got back on top. I walked in. The smell was the same as it ever was. I walked up the steps, past the pea vats, to the foreman's office, and knocked on the door. A kid answered, barely 21, bum-fluff on his chin.

"Have you got anything going?" I asked. The lad looked me up and down with disbelief. "Aren't you Don Gravy?"

"I used to be," I said. "I used to be."

AND ANOTHER THING

ON MUSIC

Music nowaways is rubbish. It's all just shouting. People say to me that "hip-hop" is poetry. It's not. It's just shouting over a beat. My son tries to tell me that "indie music" is wonderful. The lad's cracked. It's just shouting over guitars. There's not been a decent note of music played since 1987 when Steve 'Silk' Hurley's "Jack Your Body" went to Number 1 in the charts. It was all over. Mike Smith and I went to Beachy Head that Sunday night and threw all our LPs and cassettes into the sea. Not a word was spoken. We knew it was over. I listen to audio books now.

ON CRIME AND PUNISHMENT

These days we're too easy on criminals. Bring back hanging, I say. Bring back the guillotine. Bring back the firing squad. Bring back nailing criminals to a piece of hardboard, covering them in jam, and letting wasps sting them to death. It was good enough for my Grandfather's generation.

ON POLITICS

Back in 1995, before the scandal, I was approached by Peter Mandelson about running for the Labour Party in a marginal seat. Now I'd always been interested in politics, but I told Mandelson "no". I was too busy with my career. It turned out later that he'd mistaken me for another Donald Wilkins, a gentleman who I believe ran a chain of key-cutting shops in the Northampton area. Still, I wish I'd said yes. I'd probably be Prime Minister now. Then we'd see change.

ON LORD SUNDERLAND

Lord Sunderland is Britain's greatest hero. Without him, I doubt we'd have fought back the Swiss in '54. A legend.

AND ANOTHER THING

ON THE A71(M) TACKLEFORD RING ROAD

Oh the ring road! Don't get me started! Try getting past Junction 7 (for Coward Cross) between 8 and 8.30. You can't. Static. So here's my idea. Three lanes in either direction are simply not enough. I propose that the A71(M) should operate as an orbital one-way system, thereby increasing capacity to six-lanes.

Obviously, this puts drivers only wishing to travel a short distance against flow of traffic at a disadvantage, as one might have to undertake a 35-mile journey to reach the nearest junction. So on Mondays, Wednesdays and Fridays, the road will run anticlockwise. On Tuesdays and Thursdays, the road will run clockwise. At the weekends, two-way flow is restored. In this way, few are seriously disadvantaged.

Despite a dozen letters to the Departments of Transport of consecutive governments, this proposal has been criminally ignored. This country!

ON HRH PRINCE PHILLIP

Phil's a good lad. He's a mate. Even when things went south for me, he'd still call up for a chat. He's much more down to earth than you'd think. For a long time he was obsessed with Laser Tag, always tapping me up for strategies.

ON FOOD

Beef's the best meat. It just is. The cow's the only beast you'd have in your house. A chicken would be running all over the place. A pig lives in filth. A sheep... don't get me started on sheep! And as for the rest, a zoo, a bloody zoo. But cows... good people. I love eating them.

The best vegetable to eat with beef? I think I'd say the potato. Controversial nowadays, what with the popularity of rice, but I still think the potato is best. Pasta? Forget about it.

JOHN ALLISON

Born in a hidden village deep within the British Alps, John Allison came into this world a respectable baby with style and taste. Having been exposed to American comics at an early age, he spent decades honing his keen mind and his massive body in order to burn out this colonial cultural infection.

One of the longest continuously publishing independent web-based cartoonists, John has plied his trade since the late nineties moving from *Bobbins* to *Scary Go Round* to *Bad Machinery*, developing the deeply weird world of Tackleford long after many of his fellow artists were ground into dust and bones by Time Itself.

He has only once shed a single tear, but you only meet Sergio Aragonés for the first time once.

John resides in Letchworth Garden City, England and is known to his fellow villagers only as He Who Has Conquered.

— Contributed by Richard Stevens III

"THE TREASURE OF BRITANNIA"

ALSO BY JOHN ALLISON!

BAD MACHINERY, VOLUME 1:
THE CASE OF THE TEAM SPIRIT
ISBN 978-1-62010-387-6
Pocket Edition In Stores Now!

BAD MACHINERY, VOLUME 2:
THE CASE OF THE GOOD BOY
ISBN 978-1-62010-421-7
Pocket Edition In Stores Now!

BAD MACHINERY, VOLUME 3:
THE CASE OF THE SIMPLE SOUL
ISBN 978-1-62010-443-9
Pocket Edition In Stores Now!

BAD MACHINERY, VOL. 4:
THE CASE OF THE LONELY ONE
ISBN 978-1-62010-457-6
Pocket Edition In Stores Now!

BAD MACHINERY, VOL. 5:
THE CASE OF THE FIRE INSIDE
ISBN 978-1-62010-504-7
Pocket Edition In Stores Now!

BAD MACHINERY, VOL. 7:
THE CASE OF THE FORKED ROAD
ISBN 978-1-62010-562-7
Pocket Edition Coming February 2019!

ONI PRESS
www.onipress.com

bad machinery
THE CASE OF THE MODERN MEN

Coming Soon!